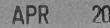

EGG-napped!

By
Marisa Montes

Illustrated by
Marsha Winborn

HarperCollinsPublishers

To my husband, David Plotkin,
for his never-ending loyalty and our
mutual love of geese and ducks
—M. M.

To S, who fills my
pictures with love
—M. W.

Egg-napped!
Text copyright © 2002 by Marisa Montes
Illustrations copyright © 2002 by Marsha Winborn
All rights reserved. Printed in Singapore. www.harperchildrens.com
Library of Congress Cataloging-in-Publication Data
Montes, Marisa (Maria Isabel).
Egg-napped! / by Marisa Montes ; illustrated by Marsha Winborn. — 1st ed.   p.   cm.
Summary: Gabbler and his wife are thrilled with their first egg and horrified when it disappears.
ISBN 0-06-028950-3. — ISBN 0-06-028951-1 (lib. bdg.)
[1. Geese—Fiction.   2. Eggs—Fiction.   3. Animals—Fiction.   4. Stories in rhyme.]
I. Winborn, Marsha, ill.   II. Title.
PZ8.3.M775 Eg   2002   99-87295   [E]—dc21
Typography by Carla Weise
1   2   3   4   5   6   7   8   9   10
❖
First edition

At the edge of the forest,
beside the goose pond,
all the animals gathered
from far and beyond
to see the arrival
of Gabbler's first egg.
"Quick! Quick!"
Gabbler called.
"Hurry up! Shake a leg!"

Gabbler strutted about;
he was puffed up with pride.
His shy wife was blushing;
she wished she could hide.

Just then Mrs. Gabbler
rose up in a hop
and out came the Egg
with a PISH! and a POP!

The animals cheered;
Gabbler honked with great zest.
"Join us now for a party—
a grand forest-fest!"
While the others were dancing
and feasting that day,
the Egg tipped and tottered
and tumbled away.

It rolled past the pond
and rolled on down the hill.
And nobody noticed. . . .
No, no one, until—

Mrs. Gabbler cried out,
"Dearie me! Dearie me!
My Egg has been Egg-napped!
Oh, how can that be?"
Poor Gabbler was frantic;
his missus was wild!
The Egg was beloved—

The Egg was their child!

"We will scour the whole wood!"
cried the flying squirrel, Kit.
"We'll search meadows and streams
and inspect every pit!"
The mice looked down low,
and the birds looked up high.
They searched and they searched—
till they heard Gabbler cry.

HEY!!

He'd spied Doris the Tortoise,
as big as a cow,
sitting next to the Egg,
with a wrinkled-up brow.

"It's MY Egg—I found it!
So don't you come near!"
But as Doris was yelling,
Kit snuck round the rear.

"IT'S OURS!" shouted Gabbler,
his wife by his side.
"It's OUR Egg you stole
and are trying to hide!"
As Doris was keeping
the parents at bay . . .

Kit pounced on the Egg,
and she rolled it away.

But Kit tripped and she slipped,
then she fell to the ground,
and the Egg rolled away
without making a sound.

It rolled down the hillside,

around an old stump,

and over the footbridge it went:
Bump!

Bump!

BUMP!

The Egg kept on rolling
and reached a high ledge,
where it teetered and tottered
right there on the edge.
"OH, NO!" Gabbler cried.
Mrs. G closed one eye.

Then suddenly something swooped down from the sky . . .

and scooped up the Egg
in its powerful claws!
Kit gave out a cheer,
and she led the applause,
but too soon . . .

for the hero was
Hector the Hawk,
who laughed, jeered, and sneered,
and then gave them a shock:
"You don't honestly think
that I saved it for *you*?
No, this Egg—is it goose?—
will taste great in a stew."

Adieu!

At that, Mrs. Gabbler
flew up in a snit:
"Give back my sweet Egg!
Give it back, you big twit!"
She flapped her wide wings
and delivered a swat,
then gave that bad hawk
a good taste of what's what!

Heh heh!

Boot!!

SQUAWK!!

His claws opened up:
Hector let the Egg go—

let it drop down

down

down

to the earth . . .

oh . . . so . . . slow. . . .

On the ground, all were screaming
and dashing about.
"Try to catch Gabbler's Egg!"
was each animal's shout.

Some ran left, some ran right;
others jumped all the while.
But the animals crashed
and collapsed in a pile.

Then the flying squirrel, Kit,
launched by someone's hind leg,
shot up high in the sky
and grabbed onto the Egg.

With all four of her paws,
tiny Kit hung on tight,

and she stretched out her flaps—

parachuting in flight.

As Kit floated to earth,
Gabbler's wings opened wide . . .
and he scooped up the Egg!
"Our Egg's safe!" his wife cried.
"We saved Gabbler's Egg!"
feisty Kit led the cheer.
"We worked as a team,
and we saved someone dear!"

On the day Gabbler's Egg
would be ready to hatch,
the animals feasted
and cheered Gabbler's catch.

Soon . . .  C^RU^NCH!

CRACK! from the Egg
popped two legs and a rear.
"Count our blessings!" cried Gabbler.

"Our Baby is here!"